W9-AZS-580

CHEER TEAM
TROUBLE

BY JAKE MADDOX

text by
Leigh McDonald

STONE ARCH BOOKS
a capstone imprint

Jake Maddox JV Girls books are published by
Stone Arch Books
a Capstone imprint
1710 Roe Crest Drive
North Mankato, Minnesota 56003
www.mycapstone.com

Cataloging-in-Publication Data is available on the Library of Congress website.
ISBN: 978-1-4965-6344-6 (library binding)
ISBN: 978-1-4965-6346-0 (paperback)
ISBN: 978-1-4965-6348-4 (eBook PDF)

Summary: Longtime gymnast Brielle decides to join a competitive cheerleading team, while
keeping her spot on the gymnastics team. She figures the practice schedules don't conflict, so she
shouldn't have any trouble managing the two sports. But things don't go as planned, and Brielle
soon finds herself pulled in too many directions.

Designer: Tori Abraham

Image Credits: Shutterstock: cluckva, 90–95 (background), Eky Studio, throughout (stripes design),
Wlg, cover (background), WoodysPhotos, cover, back cover, chapter openers

Printed and bound in the United States of America.
PA021

TABLE OF CONTENTS

CHAPTER 1

BRING IT ON

"Naomi! Wait up!" Brielle shouted across the hot parking lot. She hopped up onto the sidewalk and ran to catch up with her best friend.

Both girls had just arrived at the gym to sign up for another year of gymnastics. This year was especially exciting because they would be advancing to a regional-team level. They would compete against other gyms in the area. Brielle was looking forward to the new challenge.

She and her best friend, Naomi, had met in a parks-and-rec gymnastics class when they were in kindergarten. Soon after they had discovered that they lived only a few houses apart. They had been tumbling and cartwheeling around their backyards together ever since.

Naomi's green leotard glowed against her dark skin, and her curly black hair was held up high in a matching green band. Brielle was feeling fancy in a red leotard with a band of sequins across the chest. Her long brown hair was tucked up neatly in two French braids.

"We look like a Christmas card together," Brielle said, laughing.

She heard the car door slam behind her as her mother followed her slowly toward the front door. Brielle's happy smile turned to a sigh.

"What's wrong?" Naomi asked, bumping her shoulder into Brielle's. "Aren't you excited for gymnastics?"

"Of course I am!" Brielle explained. "But my mom is being a pain. I want to try cheer this year, like my mom and my sister did when they went to middle school."

"And your mom isn't going for it?" asked Naomi.

"My mom said OK, but she also said I had to pick just one activity! I mean, can you imagine?" Brielle continued as they walked toward the building. "I agreed to drop Scouts, because I wasn't really enjoying it much anymore anyway. And I already told her I was done with piano after the last recital. But there's no way I'm going to stop doing gymnastics with you. Especially now that we get to go to competitions! We had a big fight about it."

Naomi frowned. "You're here, though. Did you win? Or did you give up on cheer?" she asked. She glanced back and saw their moms talking to each other as they approached the building. Brielle's mom didn't look very happy, and Naomi's mom, Mrs. Robinson, was shaking her head.

"I guess I won. We agreed I could try doing both for one season and then talk about it again after that. I signed up for cheer tryouts yesterday," Brielle said. "They're on Friday."

Naomi looked at her with wide eyes as she pulled open the front door. "Wow," she said. "Do you even know what to do for cheer tryouts?"

"Well, I've been watching my sister's competitions forever, so I know what kinds of things they're looking for," Brielle said.

"Well, that's good," said Naomi.

Brielle added, "And they sent out this link to a video of routines to learn for the tryouts, so I'll practice those. Cheer uses a lot of the same skills as gymnastics, so at least I'll kind of know what I'm doing. They'll teach me the rest." She shrugged. "If I didn't even try cheer, I would always wonder if I could have been as good as my sister. She won all kinds of medals, and she's on the cheer team at college now."

Naomi smiled. "And I can come cheer you on at your competitions. Hey, there's Coach Roberts. Let's go!" The two girls raced into the lobby of the gym.

Brielle's mother came in a few moments later and walked straight over to the sign-up table. Hugging her coach hello, Brielle glanced over and noticed that her mom was frowning at the clipboard full of papers in her hand. She quickly broke away and skipped over to see what was wrong.

"I don't know, honey . . . this schedule is going to be awfully busy. Regular practice for gymnastics is Tuesdays and Thursdays, and cheer is Mondays and Wednesdays, so that's OK," her mom started. "But it looks like you'll also have a lot of weekend commitments for both. Plus you're definitely going to have more homework this year . . ."

Brielle could tell what was coming, and her heart jumped in her throat.

"I can do it, Mom!" Brielle insisted. "I can make it work! Naomi can give me rides to gymnastics stuff if it's too much for you to do it all." She glanced over at Naomi's mom, standing next to them and filling out Naomi's paperwork.

"It's fine, Carla," Mrs. Robinson said, winking at Brielle. "She's already over at our place half the time anyway. Driving two girls instead of one is no trouble."

Brielle smiled thankfully at her, then turned back to her own mom.

"And I promise I will get all of my homework done, even if I have to go to every study period at school. Please?" She bounced a little on her toes, trying hard to keep her voice even and not whiny. Whining never worked with her mother.

Brielle's mom looked her in the eyes, silent. After what felt like forever, she sighed and picked up a pen from the table.

"OK," she said, "if you really want it that badly, you can try it. But if it turns out to be too much, you're going to need to make a choice, Brielle. I know you think you can do it all but . . ." She trailed off, shaking her head.

Brielle's mom began signing the forms. Brielle threw her arms around her in a tight, thankful squeeze before skipping off again to join her friend.

When the girls went into the gym, Brielle saw a lot of new faces. She sat next to Naomi on the mat as Coach Roberts gathered them all together to begin the first practice.

"Welcome, girls," the coach said once she had everyone's attention. "As you all know, I've coached many rec teams over the years. I've enjoyed working with each of you as you've grown into the great young gymnasts that you are. Now I hope you're ready to take your skills to the next level." She paused to smile broadly at the team.

Looking around the group slowly, the coach continued, "Instead of just having fun and learning new skills, there will be a sharper focus on competition. Not only will we be competing against teams from other gyms in the area, you'll be competing against each other as well."

Competing against each other? Brielle thought. Hearing that, she exchanged a glance with her friend.

But Brielle wasn't really worried. She and Naomi would always be friends, even if they had to compete against each other.

She noticed some of the other girls looking around too, though. Suddenly they began to look a lot less friendly. A girl in a blue leotard began stretching as Coach Roberts continued talking about the details of how this new competitive team would work. Two other girls began tightening their elastic hair bands as if preparing to compete right this very moment.

Coach Roberts finished her opening speech, saying, "OK, girls, does anyone have any questions, or should we get right to work?"

Nobody raised a hand.

CHAPTER 2

T IS FOR TEAM

The week flew by, and the day of cheer tryouts arrived in a flash. Brielle was excited to test out the routines she'd been working hard on, but she was also beginning to feel a little nervous. She didn't know exactly what to expect.

The drive to the cheer gym had seemed endless as Brielle peppered her mother with questions. Her mother hadn't seemed to mind at all. She had been full of stories about her own cheer memories.

Cheerleading sounded like so much fun, but it was also hard to imagine. Who would be there? What would the coaches be like?

Brielle had watched the cheer tryout videos about a hundred times in the past week and had practiced until she could do the routines in her sleep. Now the biggest challenge was going to be acting confident and excited while performing the moves. That was going to be hard to do when her stomach was filling with butterflies.

When they went inside the lobby, she saw a sea of unfamiliar faces. She recognized a few girls from school, but there wasn't anyone there that she knew well.

It was too late to back out now, though. Brielle straightened the red bow in her high ponytail and put on her best friendly smile. She took a deep breath and walked over to the sign-in sheet. The woman behind the table smiled kindly at her.

"Hi there . . . Brielle," she said, leaning forward to look at what Brielle had written on the sheet. The woman handed her mom a clipboard with a couple of forms and asked her to fill them out before Brielle entered the gym.

Brielle looked around again at the other girls who were preparing to try out for the team. Most of them looked nearly as nervous as she felt.

She took a deep breath and tried to focus. Calm and confident. She had a strong front and back handspring, straddle jump, and other tumbling skills she had worked hard to learn.

I can do this. It's gymnastics with pom-poms and chanting, she told herself.

When the gym doors opened and the prospective team members were let in to begin the tryout, Brielle's mom squeezed her quickly and whispered, "Just breathe, and most of all, smile. You will rock this!"

Brielle forced her worried frown to melt into a cheerful grin as she walked through the open doors. It actually did make her feel a little better.

"Welcome, girls!" said a woman with a braid hanging down her back. "I am Coach Megan, and this is my assistant, Coach Jennifer." A tall woman with dark eyes and a big curly bun gave the group a friendly smile and wave. "We are excited you're here, and we can't wait to see what you can do. Who else is excited to be here? Let's hear you!"

At the prompt, all the hopeful cheerleaders started cheering and clapping. Brielle felt the excitement start to build.

"Awesome!" Coach Megan said over the crowd. Everyone quieted down as she continued. "Did everyone review the videos and come prepared to perform the routines?" The gathered girls all nodded. "Good. So who can tell me what the most important skill is in cheer?"

The girls glanced around at one another, but no one spoke. Finally a shorter girl in a purple shirt raised her hand, and the coach pointed to her. "Rhythm?" she said, sounding unsure.

"Rhythm is an important part of it, yes," the coach agreed. "That's what makes the team able to move together with each other and the music. But there's something even more important. Something no cheerleading squad can do without. Anyone else?"

"Confidence," another girl said in a loud, clear voice. Coach Megan smiled.

"Confidence is also important," she agreed. "But there is something else that all the rhythm and confidence in the world won't fix if it's missing. Any more guesses?"

The room was silent. Coach Megan waited a few seconds. "Teamwork," she finally said. "Each of you could be an amazing athlete on your own, but if you don't work well together, then the whole squad suffers."

Brielle nodded. Coach Jennifer flashed her a big smile.

"Great cheerleading squads work because of trust and teamwork. Athletic skills are wonderful, of course, but we'll also be watching how well you work with others today," Coach Megan concluded. The girls were all nodding now.

Jennifer stepped forward. "Let's warm up first," she said. The girls spread out around the gym. First they performed jumping jacks to get their hearts pumping. Then Jennifer led them through a long series of stretches.

Brielle was used to all of these stretches from gymnastics. She knew that preparing her body before beginning a routine was very important to avoid injury.

After the warm-up, the tryout began. First up was a girl named Maya. Brielle knew they went to the same school, but they had never spoken before.

At the coaches' request, Maya performed a cartwheel, front and back handsprings, and a roundoff. All of her movements were strong and clean.

Then the coaches asked her to perform a toe touch jump and a spread-eagle jump. Maya's long hair flipped above her head as she flew high into the air. She landed and smiled at the coaches, waiting patiently as they wrote on their score sheets.

"OK, Maya, whenever you're ready. Dynamite, please," Coach Megan said.

Maya cleared her throat and stepped into position to perform one of the tryout cheers.

"Our team is BOOM dynamite! Our team is BOOM dynamite!" she called out, stepping forward into a deep front lunge with a right half high V. On the word *dynamite*, she snapped back to daggers, then into ready position once more. "Our team is tick, tick, tick, tick, BOOM DYNAMITE!" Her arms flew up into a high V, then clicked downward like a ticking clock.

Brielle watched closely. She thought Maya had done a perfect job. The coaches scribbled on their clipboards for a minute, then called up each girl in turn. The second girl also did a solid performance, looking confident and excited. But the third girl didn't quite land her back handspring.

Brielle heard a couple of snickers from the back of the crowd. She looked, but she couldn't tell who they had come from. She noticed Coach Megan frowning at the group, though, and writing something down.

"Next up," the coach said after a few moments, "Brielle Johnson, please."

Brielle jumped to her feet and held her head high as she strode to the mat in front of the coaches and waited for her instructions. "Let's start with a back handspring," the coach said.

Phew, thought Brielle. *Easy.*

In fact she landed all of her tumbling tricks without any trouble, which helped her confidence rise a little bit.

Next were the jumps. The coaches requested a toe touch jump and a spirit tuck. Brielle had practiced both at home but didn't feel like they were quite ready for showing off yet. Still, she was here, and she wanted to do her best.

With a deep breath, she put a big smile on her face, making sure to look the coach in the eye. *Reach for your instep, not your toes!* Brielle thought as she leapt high into the air, her mother's reminders echoing in her head.

For the spirit tuck, as she jumped into the air again, she brought her knees up to her chest and squeezed them together as if she were pinching a coin between them.

Coach Megan made a note on her clipboard. "OK, Brielle, when you're ready, please perform the Explosion cheer," she said.

Brielle nodded and got into ready position. She smiled with a confidence she definitely did not fully feel. This was it.

"Our team is hot!" she shouted into the silent gym, stepping forward with her right foot and punching her right arm straight up. Then she snapped into a T, followed by a low touchdown pose.

"Dynamite's got nothing on us!" She lunged out with her right foot again, arms up in a bent position like she was asking a question. Then she lowered her arms in a series of short snaps as she sang out, "Let's wind it up and let it go! Explosion!" She stomped out another lunge and punch combination.

"Yeah, yeah!" she shouted, clapping. "Explosion!" She performed the final lunge and punch, finishing in a touchdown.

Suddenly the gym was very quiet, aside from the scribbling of the coaches' pens on their clipboards. Brielle could feel her heart pounding but stayed perfectly still, waiting.

Finally Coach Megan looked up again. "Great, thank you, Brielle. You may go sit down. Vivi?" she said, calling the next girl.

The coaches were being careful not to show much of a reaction on their faces as they judged the tryouts, but Brielle thought she saw a bit of a smile on Coach Jennifer's face as she took her seat.

Maya leaned over to whisper in Brielle's ear. "That was great," she said, offering her palm, which Brielle slapped quietly.

"Thanks," she said, smiling. Her heart had stopped racing, and she settled into her seat with a sigh of relief. Maybe this cheerleading thing would turn out after all.

CHAPTER 3

FLYING HIGH

When she checked the cheer team website a couple of days later, Brielle's heart jumped as she spotted her name on the list for the level four youth team.

Yes, I made it! she thought.

She was happy to see Maya's name on the list too, as well as a couple of others she remembered from tryouts. Slamming the laptop shut, she raced over to Naomi's to share her good news. She couldn't wait to tell her best friend.

When the first cheer practice rolled around, Brielle showed up ten minutes early to make sure she was totally prepared. She was glad she had, because after brief introductions and a quick warm-up, they got right down to business working on stunts.

Several of the girls who had more cheer experience were grouped together to practice some more advanced stunts. Brielle was in a group with Maya and Vivi, who were also great tumblers, but new to cheerleading. They were starting off by practicing one of the basics, a thigh stand, but it wasn't exactly a smooth start.

"OK, Maya and Vivi, you're our bases for this stunt. Now, you two stand facing each other, like this . . . ," Coach Jennifer instructed. "Brielle, you'll be our flyer. "

As Coach Jennifer talked them through the steps, the girls got into position. Maya lunged forward, matching her bent leg to her teammate Vivi's.

Brielle placed her left foot on Maya's thigh, up close to her hip, and planted her hands on both of their shoulders. At the same time, Maya grasped Brielle's foot with one hand and wrapped the other behind her knee to support it. Brielle squatted a bit to get some momentum and then pushed herself up with an "oof."

For a moment Maya winced as she took Brielle's full weight, but Brielle placed her other foot on Vivi's thigh so the weight quickly lessened. Vivi locked her hands into place around Brielle's other leg, and they were all still for a beat as Brielle tried to find her balance.

She threw her arms up in a quick V before suddenly grabbing at the two bases' shoulders again, then hopping down. Maya and Vivi stood up too. They all looked a little frustrated.

"That was a great start, girls!" Coach Jennifer said with an encouraging clap of her hands.

Brielle shook her head slightly.

Coach Jennifer put her hand on Brielle's shoulder. "Listen, we put you all on the level four team for a reason," she said. "Your tumbling and dance skills are solid, we just need a little extra work to catch you up on the stunts. I have every confidence you ladies can do this. Brielle, is there anything different you need from your bases?"

"I don't think so. You guys both did great. I don't know why I couldn't find my balance up there," she said.

"Let's try it with another spotter until you feel more comfortable," Jennifer suggested. "Emma!" She motioned to another teammate, who had been working with Coach Megan in the basket toss group. "Please come join us for a few minutes. We need a spotter."

This time as Brielle pushed herself up into the thigh stand, Emma stepped in behind her and grasped her waist firmly with both hands.

Brielle threw her arms up into a proud and solid V. This time when she hopped down, she was smiling.

"How did it feel that time?" Jennifer asked.

"Great!" Brielle said. "That was fun! Let's go again!"

After another two times practicing with Emma's support, Brielle was ready to successfully try it without a spotter. It was exciting to know she was improving.

As they were packing up at the end of practice, Maya walked over with her gym bag on her shoulder. "I have a practice room set up in my basement with mats and stuff," she said to Brielle and Vivi. "Would you guys want to come over on Saturday for some extra practice? We don't have that long before the first competition to get used to all these new stunts, so extra practice time might be a good idea."

"That would be great," Brielle said, smiling at her new friends. "I can use all the practice I can get!"

CHAPTER 4

TEAMWORK

When Brielle got home that afternoon, the sun was already low in the sky. Naomi was waiting on her front steps.

"Hey," Brielle said as she climbed out of the car. "You should have seen me today. We're putting together our first routine already, and I'm going to be a flyer!" She was excited to tell her friend about the new skills she was learning.

"Wow," Naomi said. "That sounds fun. You're getting tossed in the air?"

"Not yet," Brielle said. "More like I get to stand on people. But it's the first real stunt I've learned, and it's fun. Actual flying comes next." Then she sighed. "I can't hang out. I have to do my homework. Can you believe Mr. Miller assigned us a science project already? Maybe you can come over tomorrow?"

"We have gymnastics tomorrow," Naomi reminded her.

"Oh, yeah," Brielle said, shaking her head. "Of course. Well, at least we get to see each other and hang out there, right?"

"I guess so," Naomi said sadly. "And at the tumbling clinic on Saturday."

Brielle winced. "Oh no, I forgot about that. I promised I'd go to an extra cheer practice. We really need it . . . ," she began to explain, then trailed off. Naomi was already standing up. She obviously didn't want to hear more about cheer.

"Congratulations on the flying," she said, sounding disappointed. "See you at school, I guess."

With a wave, she slowly walked back toward her own house.

Brielle didn't know what to say. Naomi seemed pretty upset, and she felt bad about disappointing her best friend. She also couldn't believe she had forgotten about the tumbling clinic.

But before she could really muster an explanation, Naomi was already halfway to her own house. And her science project was still calling. Brielle went inside and slowly closed the door.

* * *

At the next cheer practice on Wednesday, Coach Megan watched closely as the team perfectly executed thigh stands and L stands. Brielle felt natural and safe raising her arms in a high V now with her new friends as a solid base below.

"Awesome job! All your practice is paying off. I think you girls are ready for the basket toss," the coach said.

Brielle couldn't help but give a little hop of excitement. "Yay!" she exclaimed. A basket toss was real flying!

"Brielle, let's give Maya a turn to try flyer. I'd like you to have a shot at sidespot for this one," Coach Megan said. Brielle felt a twinge of disappointment but quickly tried to hide it.

Coach Megan gave her an understanding look. "Remember, cheer is all about teamwork," she told her gently.

The coach turned to the full group. "You all need to learn as many skills as you can to make the best possible team. Stunts can't happen with a whole team of flyers," she reminded them. "Now, Trinity, please take the other sidespot position. Everyone ready?" Brielle faced Trinity, nodding, and they clasped each other's wrists.

Coach Megan took some time adjusting their stance and grip. First she moved them closer together.

"You want the point where you release your grip to be as high as possible," she explained. "The closer you are standing together, the closer your arms will be to reaching straight up, perpendicular to the ground. If you stand far apart, you can barely raise your arms at all, do you see?"

All of the girls nodded seriously as Brielle and Trinity demonstrated. Even those who weren't acting as bases yet were paying attention. They knew their turn would come.

"Great," the coach continued. "So in order to be as close together as possible without crashing, use good posture and keep your shoulders directly over your hips. Never lean forward, or you'll absorb the flyer's weight with your back." She pretended to take a sudden heavy load, bending her back in a hump like an old witch in a fairy tale.

"Instead, absorb the weight with your legs," she said, now standing tall and squatting slightly.

"Not only does this help you stay close to each other, it also protects your back from injury."

After some more discussion of the steps, the girls were ready to give it a try. Brielle and Trinity got into position, as close to each other as possible. Maya stood behind their clasped arms and placed her hands on their shoulders.

Vivi, who was back spotting, put her hands on Maya's waist. Then on the count of three, she helped her push up onto the sidespot's arms as they squatted to take her. Vivi shifted her hands to under Maya's bottom, and the three spotters threw their arms in the air as hard as possible. Maya flew!

As she fell back into her spotters' arms, Maya did her best to keep her body straight, but her left elbow flew out a little bit and knocked Brielle on the forehead as she came down. It didn't really hurt, but it did surprise her.

"Oh my gosh, I'm so sorry," Maya said as her feet hit the floor a moment later. "Did I hurt you?"

Brielle rubbed her forehead and smiled. "I'm fine," she reassured her friend. "That was nothing. You should have seen the huge bump I got when I was first learning back handsprings," she added, laughing. "Let's try it again!"

CHAPTER 5

LOSING HER COOL

Thursday morning was warm and sunny. Brielle threw her gymnastics bag in the car along with her backpack, then climbed in behind them. Her mother came out of the house a moment later, fumbling with her keys and coffee cup.

"So how's it going so far?" she asked Brielle as they were backing out of the driveway.

"Cheer is awesome," Brielle said happily. "I love it. I'm going to my friend Maya's house on Saturday for some extra practice."

She saw her mother's frown in the rearview mirror. "You are, are you? Were you planning to ask me about that? What about tumbling clinic?" she asked sharply.

Brielle groaned. "Mom," she said. "I don't need tumbling clinic as much as I need stunt practice. I can do that stuff in my sleep! But if I'm going to be a flyer in the first routine, I have a ton of work to do. And my friends need to work on it too. They can't practice without me." Her voice rose in annoyance.

"Well, it's your decision, I guess," her mother said after a moment. "I just want to make sure you're not letting gymnastics slide. You've put so much work into it already, it would be a shame for that to go to waste."

Brielle rolled her eyes. "It's not going to waste. I'm using gymnastics skills in both sports anyway," she insisted. "I've got it all under control, Mom. Stop worrying so much."

* * *

When Brielle walked into math class later that morning, though, she realized that maybe things weren't so under control. On the board were only the giant words: *QUIET, PLEASE. TESTING*. The room was as silent as a tomb.

Oh no! How could I have forgotten a math test? she thought, panicking.

When the test paper was set on the desk in front of her, the numbers swam. Brielle closed her eyes and took a deep breath, trying desperately to focus on what they'd been learning in class. It was hard to think about much beyond her shock, though. The sound of pencils busily scratching out answers all around her wasn't helping, either.

That sinking feeling stuck with her for the rest of the day. She didn't raise her hand to read aloud even once in English, although usually she loved performing in front of the class.

She barely tasted the big turkey sandwich her mother had packed for her lunch. Even while sitting in the gym waiting for Coach Roberts to begin gymnastics practice, she felt no excitement, just a vague sense of doom.

"Did you see Tessa's new leotard?" Naomi asked, sitting next to her on the mat and wiggling her long brown toes. She didn't seem to notice that Brielle wasn't in the mood to talk. When she didn't get an answer, though, Naomi turned and poked her in the ribs.

"Hello? Anyone home?" she said.

Brielle frowned. "Cut it out, Naomi," she said testily.

"Sorry," Naomi said, looking hurt. "What's wrong with you?" But before Brielle could say anything more, Coach Roberts came in.

"Our first competition is coming up, girls," the coach said, handing out papers with some information on them.

Brielle glanced at the paper, then stuck it into the side pocket of her gym bag.

"You'll be competing individually in your strongest events," Coach Roberts explained. "I'll come around today and make sure each of you knows what routine to work on and the details of what to expect. We need everything nailed down by next practice."

Brielle tried to throw herself into practice, hoping that maybe moving her body would help get the blown math test off her mind.

What if it's not as bad as I think it is, she began to wonder hopefully. *Maybe I did OK, and I just feel like I didn't because I was so surprised.* Just then her foot came down too far to one side on the balance beam, and she nearly tumbled off.

Coach Roberts looked over from across the gym, where she was helping a girl named Anna polish her routine on the bar. As Brielle regained her balance, the coach called out, "I'll be there in a minute, Brielle. Take it easy."

The coach turned back to the bars as Anna finished her swing and dropped to the mat with a clean landing. They began talking intently.

Brielle sighed and began practicing a beam handstand again—by herself. Since gymnastics had become competitive, it seemed like the coach was spending more and more time with the two or three very best gymnasts, and the rest of them had to fight for any help or attention at all.

After another couple of wobbly attempts, Brielle looked over to the mats where Naomi was practicing her floor routine. Her friend's brow was wrinkled with concentration. She raised her arms, then set off into a series of tumbling moves that took her all the way across the floor.

She's getting really good, Brielle thought.

Just then Coach Roberts walked over and began talking to Naomi, moving her hands as she demonstrated some pointers on Naomi's back handspring.

So much for coming to me next! Brielle thought with irritation.

She hopped off the beam and stomped off to get some water. More than anything, she was just ready for this day to be over.

CHAPTER 6

JUGGLING

By Monday, Brielle was feeling more like herself again. After school, she nearly flew out the door to cheer practice. She couldn't wait to show the coaches the skills she and her new cheer friends had practiced at Maya's on Saturday. Learning to be a flyer was hard work, but it was also a lot of fun.

They were working on adding express ups to their routine, and the stunt was really tricky. As flyer, Brielle had to place her foot in the base's hold, then push up on their shoulders like usual.

But instead of keeping the first leg as her landing leg, the bases tossed her as she switched legs on the way up. Then they were supposed to catch the second foot as she came down and hold her steady. They had managed it a couple of times, but were still doing a lot more falling than hitting the mark.

She understood now what Coach Megan had meant when she talked about trust being such an important part of teamwork, the key to success in a cheerleading squad. It took a lot of trust to let people lift or even throw your whole body in the air and believe that they would catch you safely.

The bases and spotters also had to trust that the flyer would do her part to stay tight and balanced in the act. One wrong move on anyone's part could cause real injury.

At the end of practice, Coach Megan gathered all of the cheerleaders on the bleachers with a few minutes left to go.

"Our first competition is in three weeks, on Saturday afternoon. I'll email the details to your parents," she said. "I want you all there an hour early to give you time to get ready without rushing, OK?" Everyone nodded solemnly. "You've all been working so hard. You should be very excited to get up on that stage so everyone can see what a fantastic team you are!"

* * *

As the days toward the competition ticked on, Brielle poured her heart into being a great cheer teammate. Gymnastics practice was demanding too, though, especially with their first meet coming soon. Although she had been working hard, her routine had a couple of skills in it that still needed a lot of work.

She was especially struggling with her cartwheel to a side handstand on the beam. She had practiced and practiced with the wall and booster blocks to get the quarter-turn dismount.

When she tried it on a real beam, though, she couldn't seem to time the twist right. Once she had even banged her shoulder on the beam pretty hard on the way down and earned herself a big yellow bruise.

But as hard as she was working at gymnastics, she was more worried about cheer. If she messed up in gymnastics, she wasn't going to hurt anyone else. In cheer, though, it wasn't only about a score. She had to be there for her teammates no matter what.

Unfortunately giving her all in two demanding sports didn't leave much time or energy for caring about anything else. One Friday in English class, their teacher, Mr. Pullman, told them about a big new assignment. It was a five-page essay, the longest any of them had ever had to write before. They were going to have two weeks to work on it.

Walking out of class, Maya caught up with Brielle in the hallway. "Want to come over again after our extra practice tomorrow morning?" she asked. "I'm inviting Vivi and Emma too."

Brielle hesitated. "I'm not sure if I have time," she said. "I also have a tumbling clinic for gymnastics in the afternoon, and I can't miss it. I already skipped the last one, and we have a competition coming up."

"Oh. Well, if you decide you can, let me know," Maya said, heading off to her Spanish class. Brielle walked slowly toward math class. She really wanted to hang out with her new friends, but how could she fit it all in? Maybe if she got up early and worked on the essay in the morning, she could make it work.

As she sat down in math class, she suddenly realized the entire room was silent. The teacher, Ms. Janome, was walking slowly up the rows handing everyone a piece of paper. Brielle's heart sank. It was their test!

She'd mostly put it out of her mind since that terrible day, but it had still been there, worrying at her during quiet moments. Now she didn't have to wonder anymore. The paper was handed to her face down, and she took a deep breath before flipping it over.

C-minus! Her heart sank. She'd never gotten a C-minus on anything before in her life!

At lunch she stared at her sandwich as Naomi talked about her routine in the upcoming gymnastics competition. She was so lost in thought that she was only half listening. Finally she heard Naomi say impatiently, "Hey, what's up with you?"

"Sorry," Brielle said. "I forgot about the math test last week, and I bombed it. And now I'm also kind of freaking out about this essay we have to write for English too. It's due right before the next cheer competition."

Naomi nodded. "Oh, yeah, Mr. Pullman gave us that essay in our class too. I'm going to the library to research tomorrow before the tumbling clinic. You want to come with me?"

Brielle sighed. "I can't. We have an extra cheer practice because of the competition in two weeks," she explained.

"Two weeks?" Naomi said, frowning. "What day?"

"Saturday. In the afternoon. Why?" Brielle asked, halfway distracted by thoughts of squeezing in that English essay.

"Two weeks from Saturday is the first gymnastics competition too. Did you forget?" Naomi asked, her voice rising. Brielle looked at her, startled. Naomi's cheeks were flushed.

"What? That's Sunday!" she said, racking her brain to remember what the coach had said.

"No. It's Saturday morning. Over at the high school gym in Centerville," Naomi said. "You're going to be there, right?" she said.

"Of course I am," Brielle insisted, her heart pounding. She'd just have to find a way to do both competitions in one day. There was no other choice.

CHAPTER 7

COMPETITION CRUNCH

Brielle's bare feet landed on the mat with a solid thump, and she tossed her arms high as the music ended. That was it. She'd just completed her first gymnastics competition.

Her cartwheel had been a little shaky, but she hadn't fallen. Judging by the loud cheering that had erupted from the bleachers behind her, she'd actually done OK. Now she just had to patiently wait for her score to be announced.

As she headed off the floor and back toward her team, she saw her teammates were clapping too, but some didn't look very happy about it. The individual competition was fierce. Coach Roberts was the only one who truly seemed excited for her.

Even Naomi's smile seemed forced, and she looked away quickly. *Although that isn't so unusual anymore,* Brielle realized sadly. Feeling a little hurt, she sat down at the other end of the bench.

As the next competitor took the floor, Brielle glanced nervously at the clock above the judges' table. The cheer competition started in just a couple of hours.

She had assured both coaches that she would be able to handle it, but she was only going to have about a half an hour to get across town. And she had to be ready to perform all over again. There wasn't a second to spare.

* * *

In the car, Brielle wiggled out of her lucky red gymnastics leotard and into her cheer uniform. It was red and blue, with a big shiny star on the chest. She pulled several bobby pins out of her hair, and slipped a blue scrunchie over the elastic to turn her bun into a high ponytail.

"Almost there! I'll just have to fix your makeup in the parking lot real quick," her mother said, shouting a little over the radio.

As she entered the gym a few minutes later, Brielle saw her team gathered around Coach Megan, who had already begun her pep talk. She jogged over, panting, and joined the group. Maya reached back and squeezed her arm. "There you are!" she whispered, sounding relieved.

Their team was the third to perform in the competition. When the second team had jogged off the stage, they heard the announcer boom, "And now, please welcome Cheer Force One!"

This was it. Together the girls jogged onto the stage with big smiles and took up a ready position in a large triangle formation. Then the music began.

The lights glittered in her eyes as Brielle ran out onto the stage with her cheer team. She blinked and tried to keep the smile on her face as big as possible.

She had been too keyed up with nerves and excitement to sleep well the night before. And after the morning's gymnastics competition, her body was exhausted. Now, as she danced across the stage, the audience looked like it was swimming.

Still things went well at first. Despite her exhaustion, Brielle was keeping up with the team. She leaped into a front handspring series across the stage, then turned and readied for the combination jumps. First she went up onto her toes, arms high in the air. Then she leaped up three times, rotating a bit with each jump. First was a pike, then a hurdler, and finally a double toe touch.

When she finished, she was facing Maya and Vivi, who had rotated the other way. They nodded and quickly got into position for the express up. Behind them, two other groups were preparing for the same stunt.

Brielle took a deep breath and readied herself behind the bases. She planted her foot firmly in their grasp, and on the count, she pushed up. Maya and Vivi tossed her as high as they could, and she switched legs right on cue. Her landing foot was too far forward, though, and her toes missed the catch.

Suddenly she was falling down into the cradle well ahead of the other flyers, who had hit their marks and were standing proud and high above their spotters.

She heard Vivi groan in frustration as she pushed her back to her feet. There was no time to dwell on the mistake, though. The team moved into the dance formation before the next stunt.

Brielle tried hard to stay focused. She threw her arms in the air in unison with the girls on either side, then swiveled into a series of cartwheels, ending up as one point of a star formation. She jumped high in a double toe touch before realizing that she had somehow missed a step. No one else was jumping.

Leaving the stage, she stared at her feet. She didn't even want to make eye contact with anyone. She felt an arm go around her shoulders, though, and finally looked up. Coach Megan was standing beside her, talking to the team.

"You all worked really hard out there, girls. You really nailed some very hard stunts! Great job," she said cheerfully. "Kate, that liberty was rock solid," she added. "Nice work."

Then she leaned down to Brielle, and said softly, "Can you please stay for just a minute afterward?"

Brielle felt her throat choke and tears well in her eyes. All she could do was nod.

For the rest of the competition, Brielle couldn't even look at the rest of her cheerleading team. She shrank lower and lower in her seat as the minutes marched by.

CHAPTER 8

DECISIONS, DECISIONS

Tap, tap, tap, tap, tap. Brielle's shoes knocked out a rhythm on the floor as she stared blankly at her gym bag. Her mistakes played over and over in her head as she waited for Coach Megan. She couldn't block them out. She wondered if they would haunt her sleep that night.

Finally the rest of the team trickled out of the locker room, and Coach Megan came over and sat down beside her. She looked at Brielle's tapping feet, then at her worried face.

"What I saw today wasn't close to what I normally get from you, Brielle," she said gently. "Did the crowd make you nervous? Or the competition? Tell me what's going on."

Feeling embarrassed, Brielle looked around to check for listening ears, but the only other cheerleaders left in the locker room were talking to each other in the far corner. She sighed.

Maybe she could just go with Coach Megan's suggestion and blame nerves. She didn't really want to talk about all the pressure she had been feeling.

But then again, maybe it would help to talk to someone, and who else did she have to talk to? Naomi was barely speaking to her lately, and her cheer teammates weren't exactly knocking down the door to hang out either. She definitely didn't want to talk to her mother about it. Not after she had insisted that she could handle being on two teams and starting middle school at the same time.

She realized Coach Megan was still sitting there, waiting for her to speak. "It's just that it's so much at once," she said slowly. "I'm not only on this team, I'm also on a competitive gymnastics team. We had a big competition this morning." She paused for a moment. It was more than just the events, she realized. "And I'm spending so much time at practices that I'm totally bombing everything important at school too. I don't know what to do," she concluded.

"Why didn't you come to me about this sooner," Coach Megan asked, putting her arm around Brielle's shoulders. "You know I'm here to help you, right?"

"Yeah . . . ," Brielle started. She was totally overwhelmed, and it was time to admit it. "Maybe I can't stay on both teams," she said suddenly, tears filling her eyes. "Sorry," she added, sniffling.

Coach Megan got up and grabbed some tissues for her from the bathroom area, then settled down again on the bench.

Now I'm crying in the locker room! This is so embarrassing, Brielle thought miserably as she grabbed a tissue.

She glanced over at the other cheerleaders, ready to run to the bathroom and hide. But they were still fixing their hair and chattering away like nothing was happening at all. She took a deep breath and blew it out.

"It sounds like you've been under a lot of stress. Is this your first year doing two sports at once?" Coach Megan asked.

Brielle shook her head. "I did soccer before, but it wasn't nearly as much work as cheer," she said. "I thought it would be the same, that it would be easy to manage. But it isn't at all," she said, sighing. Then she straightened up and looked her coach in the eyes, alarmed. "But I love cheer! I really, really love it. I don't want to quit. I just . . ." She trailed off, slumping over again.

Coach Megan looked thoughtful for a minute. "Let me tell you something," she said finally. "I've had a similar problem before."

Brielle looked at her, surprised. "You did competitive gymnastics and cheerleading too?"

"No . . . my problem wasn't with gymnastics and cheer," the coach said, smiling, "but with trying to do too much at once. I was in a band, and I started coaching the cheer team, and then I got a new job, and . . . well, I won't bore you with the details, but let's just say I learned my lesson. When you start spreading yourself too thin, it's impossible to do anything very well. Even if you could be good at each one of those things on its own. Does that sound familiar?"

Brielle nodded again. That was exactly the problem. She was good at gymnastics, and she knew she was on her way to being great at cheer too. And she had always loved school. But together, it felt like it was all falling apart.

"But what did you do about it?" she asked. "How did you decide what to give up?"

Coach Megan replied, "Tell me what you like about these two sports."

Brielle thought for a minute. "Well," she began slowly, "my best friend, Naomi, and I have been doing gymnastics together forever. It's always been our favorite thing to do. Even when we're not at practice, we love to tumble and mess around at her house or mine."

"I had a cheer friend like that when I was growing up," said Coach Megan. "We had so much fun together."

"Naomi and I used to have fun too," said Brielle. "But this year, we started on a competitive team, and that was more weird than fun. Everyone is so focused on getting ahead as an individual. There's hardly any team spirit at all."

Coach Megan nodded. "And what about cheer?"

Brielle smiled. "Cheer is the best!" she said. "I always knew my mom and sister loved it, but it turned out to be even better than I expected."

"I'm glad to hear that!" Coach Megan smiled warmly. "What do you love about it?"

Brielle sat up straighter in her chair. "I love that I get to use my gymnastics skills, but I also get to do stunts. Everyone has to work so hard together on those or else the stunt falls apart. It's really hard work sometimes, but I love it." She paused, and her face clouded again. "Except when I let everyone down because I'm so busy and tired all the time. That's a horrible feeling," she added.

Coach Megan watched her carefully. "It sounds to me like you enjoy cheer a lot. And I know you have a lot of spirit. I might be biased, but you sound less excited about gymnastics. Do you think maybe what you like most about gymnastics now is that it's a part of your friendship with Naomi?"

Brielle nodded slowly. She hadn't thought about it that way before, but maybe Coach Megan was right. She hadn't really been enjoying gymnastics that much lately. It just felt important because she had always done it with her best friend. But why couldn't they still do gymnastics together, even if she wasn't on the team anymore?

"It's weird to think about not being on a team together anymore. We have been together since kindergarten!" she finally said aloud.

Coach Megan smiled. "But you'll still be friends, right? And just think—if you're not doing the same sport, you don't have to compete. You can just cheer each other on. I know it's not the same, but it could still be fun."

"That's actually what Naomi said when I told her I was joining cheer in the first place," Brielle remembered, smiling. "About cheering me on, I mean."

She felt nervous about the idea of telling Naomi and her coach she wanted to quit gymnastics, but the more she thought about it, the more it felt like the right decision. In fact, she suddenly felt better than she had in weeks. Having time to focus on school and cheer sounded amazing.

Brielle knew what she had to do.

CHAPTER 9

BREAKING UP IS HARD TO DO

Brielle sat outside Naomi's house, her feet tapping nervously on the sidewalk. Telling her mother about her decision had been easy. Her mom had thought cheer on top of gymnastics might be too much from the very beginning, although Brielle was thankful she hadn't pointed that out when she broke the news.

Mom had just given her a hug and said, "I know it must have been a very hard decision, but I'm proud of you, honey. Sometimes the right choice isn't the easiest."

Telling Coach Roberts had been a lot harder. She had invited Brielle to be a part of the competitive team after coaching her for many years. She was disappointed that Brielle was choosing to drop out now. But still, she had understood. And Brielle had felt a million times better once she had made that phone call.

But now she was waiting for Naomi to come home so that she could tell her in person, and her stomach was full of butterflies.

What if Naomi doesn't want to be friends anymore? She pushed that thought away as quickly as it had come. That was silly—of course Naomi would still be her friend. They had a lot more between them than a gymnastics team.

She watched Mrs. Robinson's familiar blue sedan turn the corner at the end of the street and then pull into the driveway. Mrs. Robinson smiled and gave her a little wave, but Naomi got out of the car warily.

"What's up?" she asked, frowning a little. Brielle stood up and smiled nervously.

"I just wanted to talk to you for a minute. Can I come in?" she explained.

"Sure, I guess," Naomi said. They waited for Mrs. Robinson to unlock the door, then headed straight to Naomi's room. Brielle flopped on the bed like she had done a million times before, then sat up again, feeling awkward. Naomi sat next to her, tossing her book bag on the floor with a thump.

"So . . . ," Brielle began. She took a deep breath, her stomach knotting. *There's no way out but through*, she told herself. *Just say it.* "First I wanted to tell you that I'm sorry I've been so weird lately. It's not you. It's just that trying to keep up in gymnastics and cheer and school all at the same time got crazy. I was losing it," she explained. Naomi nodded but didn't speak. "So I decided . . . I'm leaving the gymnastics team." Brielle said the final words quickly.

Naomi looked surprised for a moment, opening and closing her mouth a couple of times before she finally spoke. "But you're going to still do cheer?" she asked.

"Yeah," Brielle said. "I really like it. I still get to do some gymnastics skills, but there is so much more. And I don't want to let my team down. I love being part of a team." She peered at Naomi, her eyes tearing up a little bit. "But I don't need to do gymnastics to be your best friend . . . right?" she added, her voice beginning to choke.

"Of course not!" Naomi said, frowning. There was silence for a long, painful moment. Then she looked at Brielle and threw her arms around her in a hug. "I'm just gonna miss you over there. Like, really miss you."

"I'm pretty sure you're the only one," Brielle said.

"Yeah, those other girls are so serious about everything," Naomi agreed. "But it definitely won't be the same without you."

After a moment, Naomi sighed and fell back onto the bed. "I'm sorry I was being weird too," she added. "This year has been hard so far. I thought you were just getting to be better friends with your cheer friends and didn't need me anymore."

"No!" Brielle said. "I mean, I have made new friends there. But you'll always be my best friend. We'll just have some different tricks to show each other now. Right?"

"Right. And you'll come cheer me on too . . . I mean, when you can. After all, you'll be a cheer expert now," Naomi said, smiling.

Brielle smiled too. "I wouldn't miss it," she said.

* * *

Cheer on Monday felt like a whole new world. Brielle couldn't help bouncing as she walked into the gym. With so much pressure gone and her focus set on cheer, she felt ready to take this sport by storm.

Her excitement must have showed, because Coach Jennifer commented twice on her great facials during the dance part of practice. Her tumbling hit the mark every time. And when it was time to work on stunts, she felt ready to soar.

"OK, girls," Coach Megan instructed. "Please split into your groups for the express up."

Maya and Vivi and a few other spotters gathered around Brielle. Behind them, two other groups were preparing for the same stunt. Brielle smiled, imagining the parts of the move. When everyone was in place, she readied herself behind the bases and planted her foot firmly in their grasp.

"Five, six, seven, eight," Maya chanted, and she pushed up with a fluid motion.

Maya and Vivi tossed her as high as they could, and she switched legs right on cue. Her landing foot came down, and she felt their hands wrap around her foot and calf in a strong, solid hold. She raised her arms in a triumphant V, grinning madly.

Then she was falling down into the cradle in a smooth dismount and hopping back onto the floor with her teammates.

"Awesome, Brielle!" Vivi was shouting. "That was a perfect ten!"

Maya threw her arm around Brielle's shoulder for the first time in weeks. Coach Megan clapped her hands and said, "Excellent, girls. Now let's see if you can repeat that, OK?"

"Absolutely!" Brielle exclaimed. "Let's do this!"

Over the next fifteen minutes, they only missed the stunt once. A huge improvement since the last competition.

At the end of practice, Coach Megan gathered them all on the bleachers with a few minutes left to go. "Now that you've had a chance to work off the last competition, I wanted to talk to you about the next one we're preparing for. It's a big one. If we win a top spot in this competition," she explained, "we'll be invited to regionals."

Coach Jennifer began handing out papers to everyone as Coach Megan explained, "Here are some of the details you'll need to prepare. Please take this information home and share it with your parents. We'll be traveling to Scottsboro and staying in a hotel since it's a two-day event. Chaperones are, of course, welcomed and needed."

Brielle looked at the paper in her hand. This competition would be held the first weekend in December. That sounded like a long time from now, but she knew they had a lot of work to do. She carefully folded the paper and stuffed it into the side pocket of her gym bag.

On the way out, Brielle stuffed her bag as quickly as possible and caught up with Maya and Vivi. "Hey, so do you guys want to come over on Saturday? Watch a movie or something?" she asked. They looked surprised but nodded.

"You don't have to do gymnastics or something?" Maya asked.

"Nope," Brielle said. "All cheer all the time from now on."

"Cool," Vivi said. "A movie would be awesome."

"You don't mind if I invite my friend Naomi too, do you?" Brielle added. "I think you guys will really like each other."

"Sure!" Maya said, smiling. "Can't wait to meet her!"

Brielle sang as she ran out to her mom's car, her ponytail swinging. "Our team is BOOM, dynamite!"

CHAPTER 10

TEAM TRIUMPH

"And now, please welcome to the Youth Level Four competition stage . . . Cheer Force One!" the announcer boomed.

The cheer team's music mix started up as the audience cheered. Brielle danced out onto the floor alongside her teammates. Big smiles glowed on every face, and their shiny red and blue uniforms sparkled under the lights. It was showtime, and they were ready to go.

Once in position, Brielle punched left, right, and swung around in a full circle, hair flipping wildly. Behind them, Emma and four other girls were performing an impressive double down for their first stunt.

As their teammate spiraled in the air, Brielle and four others flipped into two back handsprings into a back tuck. She landed in near-perfect unison with the other tumblers as several others began flipping forward into a layout. Then they gathered into three groups for a coordinated express up to a tick-tock.

Brielle was in the center group as flyer. In rehearsals this stunt had been strong. But she felt a flicker of nerves as she remembered this was her first competition performing as a flyer since the last disaster.

Shaking off the bad memory, she planted her hands firmly on Maya and Vivi's shoulders and waited for the count.

"Five, six, seven, eight!" she heard, and suddenly she was launching into the air, hopping from foot to foot as the bases and spotters below caught her in their solid grasp. She raised her arms in a high V, and suddenly her eyes fell on a familiar face a few rows back in the crowd—Naomi. Brielle felt her big grin get even bigger as Maya and Vivi launched her into kick single basket toss and back to the floor.

The girls tumbled apart into a new formation, hearts pounding. Brielle had felt good going into this competition. They'd worked hard, harder than she'd ever worked before. But now, on stage and full of energy, everything was coming together even better than she'd hoped.

After another round of jumps and stunts, they slammed into the dance portion of their routine. Brielle felt the music carry her along to the final pose, and suddenly it was over. They waved as they jogged off the stage, smiling at the audience and the judges.

Backstage, they gathered in a happy heap around their coaches. "Amazing, girls," Coach Megan said. "You should be extremely proud. I saw every bit of your hard work on that stage tonight." She winked at Brielle. "I think those were some of the cleanest stunts I've seen from you yet! Way to go the extra mile when it really counts, ladies." Brielle beamed.

After they'd taken their first-place awards back to the hotel, Brielle and her teammates changed into their regular clothes and headed back down to the lobby with their bags. The hotel hallways rang with their excited chatter.

"We're headed for regionals!" Vivi called out. "I can't believe it!"

"Team party at my house!" Maya sang.

As they passed through the front doors and into the parking lot, Brielle saw Naomi and her mom standing near the team bus. She quickly slung her bag into the hold with the others and ran over to hug them.

"I can't believe you drove all the way out here!" she said, grinning. "After watching us, are you ready to join cheer too?"

"I think I'll stick with gymnastics," Naomi said, smiling. "But I couldn't miss watching you! First place! You killed it!"

"Ice cream?" Mrs. Robinson asked with a wink.

"I have to ride the bus home," Brielle said, "but when we get back to town, you're on."

She scrambled up into the bus, waving through the window at her best friend before she plopped into a seat between two of her new ones. Win or lose, being part of the team was the best feeling of all.

ABOUT the AUTHOR

Leigh McDonald loves books! Whether she is writing them, reading them, editing them, or designing their covers, books are what she does best. She lives in a colorful bungalow in Tucson, Arizona, with her husband, Porter, her two daughters, Adair and Faye, and two big, crazy dogs, Roscoe and Rosie.

GLOSSARY

base (BAYSS)—in cheerleading, the person who remains in contact with the floor and lifts the flyer into a stunt

commitment (kuh-MIT-mint)—a promise to do something

chaperone (SHAP-uh-rohn)—someone, such as a teacher or parent, who goes with children on a trip or to an event to make sure that the children behave well and stay safe

clinic (KLI-nik)—a meeting during which a group of people learn about a particular thing or work on a particular problem or skill

flyer (FLY-uhr)—in cheerleading, the person who is elevated into the air by the bases; the person who is on top of a pyramid/stunt

muster (MUSS-tihr)—to work hard to find or get courage, support, etc.

rhythm (RITH-uhm)—a regular beat in music, poetry, or dance

spotter (SPOT-uhr)—in cheerleading, a person who watches for any hazards in the stunt; the person responsible for watching the flyer and who must be prepared to catch her/him if she/he falls

squad (SKWAHD)—a group of people who work as a team to achieve a goal

stunt (STUHNT)—in cheerleading, any skill or feat involving tumbling, mounting, a pyramid, or toss

tumbling (TUHM-bling)—any gymnastic skill used in a cheer, dance, or for crowd appeal

DISCUSSION QUESTIONS

1. Throughout the story, Brielle struggles with feeling overcommitted to her activities and schoolwork. Have you ever felt this way? Compare your experiences with Brielle's. How did you overcome your problem?

2. The gymnastics team changes for Brielle and Naomi and becomes competitive for the first time. Using examples from the story, talk about some of the benefits of competitive sports. What are some of the downfalls?

3. Coach Megan asks Brielle questions to help her decide what to do. Has an adult ever helped you make a hard decision? Who was it? What did they say that was helpful to you? Have you ever listened when a friend was having a hard time?

WRITING PROMPTS

1. Brielle had a hard time managing her schedule. If she wrote down her commitments, it could help her keep things straight. Write a schedule for your whole week, including anything you are committed to attend, such as team practice, family dinner, or school.

2. Naomi surprises Brielle and shows up at her competition. Write a thank you card from Brielle to Naomi. What do you think Brielle would want her best friend to know about how she feels?

3. Brielle has to make a hard decision between two things she enjoys doing. A pro-con list can sometimes help in making these choices. Write two lists like this to help Brielle decide between gymnastics and cheer. In the pro column for each sport, write what Brielle likes about it. In the con column, write what she doesn't like.

PREVENTING INJURY

For such a high-energy sport, cheerleading has a surprisingly low rate of injury. However, any demanding physical activity does have some risks. Ligament sprains, muscle strains, and even concussions and fractures can happen to cheerleaders of all experience levels.

Studies show that most competitive cheerleading injuries happen during practice. But some basic safety measures can help you practice responsibly and lessen or even prevent injuries.

- Always warm up and cool down at the beginning and end of practice.

- Stretch regularly to help prevent muscle strains, which are caused by moving a muscle too quickly and forcefully.

- Train at a steady pace, and avoid trying to do too much before your body is ready. Listen to your coach or trainer; they can advise you on what stunts and moves you are ready to handle.

- Train only in a dedicated space with no tripping or slipping hazards.

- Use enough spotters for stunts, and place mats on the floor or ground to reduce the impact of any falls.

- If your training area doesn't have enough vertical room for a safe throwing stunt, scale down your routine to fit the space available.

- Wear shoes with proper foot and ankle support.

- Practice proper techniques for landing, using stable positions that protect your knees and ankles.

- Wear additional hand, knee, or wrist braces if you have a known issue with any of these joints.